W.C. M'Kinnon

The Papacy

SALZWASSER
VERLAG

W.C. M'Kinnon

The Papacy

Reprint of the original, first published in 1859.

1st Edition 2022 | ISBN: 978-3-37512-222-5

Verlag (Publisher): Salzwasser Verlag GmbH, Zeilweg 44, 60439 Frankfurt, Deutschland
Vertretungsberechtigt (Authorized to represent): E. Roepke, Zeilweg 44, 60439 Frankfurt, Deutschland
Druck (Print): Books on Demand GmbH, In de Tarpen 42, 22848 Norderstedt, Deutschland

THE PAPACY:

THE SACRIFICE OF THE MASS.

THIRD LECTURE,

DELIVERED BEFORE THE PROTESTANT ALLIANCE,

OF NOVA SCOTIA.

AT TEMPERANCE HALL, HALIFAX, ON TUESDAY EVENING,
JANUARY 11th, 1859.

BY REV. W. C. M'KINNON.

HALIFAX, N. S.:
PRINTED AT THE WESLEYAN CONFERENCE STEAM PRESS.
1859.

THE SACRIFICE OF THE MASS.

BY REV. W. C. M'KINNON.

WE are met to consider, not the errors of the Church of Rome taken as a whole, but rather to gaze on one particular feature of that gigantic system, bearing the name of " THE PAPACY." Did one holy influence proceed from that system —did one ray of God's own light mingle with the darkness which envelopes the Man of Sin—were one stream of the river of life mingling with the great current of Papal abomination—I question if I should be found engaged under these circumstances. But the whole system is corrupt : the stream is tainted, the darkness is without any mixture of light ; and I feel myself in my appropriate place to-night, when attempting to delineate the evils of that great system of error and misrepresentation.

It has been said that the devil can counterfeit, but that he cannot invent. So is this true of the Papacy : she can counterfeit—she cannot invent. She has moulded herself on the Church of Christ, and is yet a cheat and a deception.

It were a pitiable object to see a giant pelted—yet putting forth efforts for his deliverance worthy of a giant. With what commiseration would we be disposed to regard the Titan, who thus should make effort after effort to arise from the earth, and not be successful.

Such is the pitiable condition of the Redeemer's Church. She is making a giant effort to throw off the incubus of that system which has been created by Satanic cunning during the long ages of the past. Will she be successful? Shall *we* see the solution of the problem? Shall we behold that day when she shall stand forth as the triumphant victor over her adversary, now grasping her as another Laocoom? Time gives the reply.

All is darkness where the Church has not lit her torch. The earth without the light of christianity, is as dark as *Rome* herself.

> " The double night of ages, and of her
>   Night's daughter Ignorance, hath wrapt and wrap
> All round us: we but feel our way to err:
> The ocean hath its chart—the stars their map,
> And knowledge spreads them in her ample lap;
> But Rome is as the desert: where we steer
> Stumbling o'er recollections now we clap
> Our hands and cry " *Eureka*" it is clear,
> When but some false mirage of ruin rises near."

Take from man the light of christianity, and again the earth is involved in gloom intense and intolerable. Wherever moral light has dawned, the light has been shed abroad through the heavenly atmosphere of the Christian Church. Wherever the stagnant pools of the depths of human thought have been stirred to their fountains, the Christian Church has strung the plummet. Wherever the good salt has preserved corrupt humanity from pollution, the Christian Church has sown that salt. Wherever there has been maintained a warfare with error, superstition and spiritual death, the Christian Church has maintained that warfare. She has enlightened the world and blessed humanity.

Now what shall we say of a system which, pretending to afford light, has only made the darkness more intolerable. Of a system which pretending to lead man to a higher spiritual condition, has only succeeded in wrapping around the human

soul the swaddling bands of a darkness so dense as to be
impenetrable. Of a system which pretending to wage war
with the hosts of darkness, has made common cause with the
enemy. The defection of a legion to the enemy's camp, is not
comparable for evil to the existence of one spy within that
camp. The defection of the first might be deplored : but it
could be remedied. But the evils wrought by the other could
not be remedied ; the results must flow on uncontrolled.
Thus stands Rome the great impediment to the spread of the
Redeemer's Kingdom.

The light which has been refracted and broken from stained
glass is still light. The rays which have transpierced the
dim clouds, are still rays of the solar fire. But the light
which falls upon the planet, is only reflected from that side of
the planet which is nearest to the sun. We all may remem-
ber Milton's lovely image of the cloud which turned her silver
lining to the moon—and whilst all is dark below, all is light
above. But with Rome, if the light be shed upon her from
above, it is absorbed in her. She neither presents light to
God, as being received from him—nor to man, as communi-
cated. The system is darkness itself. And that darkness is
only rendered the more awful, when occasionally the flash of a
Massillon's genius or piety, sends its lightning ray over the
storm clouds of gathering intense gloom, which roll from far
in the valleys below.

It were a revolting sight to gaze on a corpse, which rose,
dressed, sat down to table, rose up, knelt in prayer, extended
its ghastly hand, walked the streets, and yet spake not a
syllable, but continued a loathsome corpse. Such is Rome.
She is a corpse! A mass of spiritual corruption—a giant
crushing all that is holy and unearthly down—but retaining
the pallid face, the ghastly eye, the skeleton hand, the mute
tongue, of one who had emerged from the darkness and
corruption of the grave! But that figure, say you, is a

vampire. And what is a vampire? That which feeds on blood and destroys human victims! If the system of the Papacy were quenched by the spirit of life—if a living soul were breathed therein—then might we be brought to respect that system which, as now exhibited, is a mass of spiritual death. And the Church of Rome is an apostate Church. Had half Christendom gone over to infidelity, it would not have equalled the evil produced by the existence of one apostate Church—a Church which, while pretending to be the supporter of the religion of Jesus, and the defender of that is virtuous and pure, is only the fierce and inveterate enemy of Christ's plan, and the foul justifier of the system which is misnamed the Redeemer's Church.

Such is the position occupied by the Church of Rome. You look for water from the dark cloud which expands above the thirsty earth, and seems about bursting from its very repletion, and bitter is the mockery on the part of the deceived watcher as it passes on, and nothing is produced, save the promise unfulfilled. The traveller expects to lave his parched lips when he catches far off in the desert's sand, the appearance of the chrystal fount. Bitter must be his vexation to find that "but a mirage mocked his eye." The shrinking human soul looks for sympathy from the friends to whose bosom he confides the tale of his sorrows. How great his grief, to perceive that tale only made the subject of derision, and that by the friends who loved him but in profession. And on this principle we act. What is expected from a Church which gives the promise of truth and yet presents falsehood? What of a church which professes to give light, and yet gives darkness? What of a Church which promises salvation, and yet leads men to perdition? Yet such is Rome. Rome, the gradual developement of ages of superstition. Rome, the embodiment of the false and the beautiful —the weak and the strong. Rome, the result of ceaseless

efforts of the "man of sin" to perpetuate his image in man.
Rome, the master-piece of satan—the opposer of Christ—the
deformed monster of theology—the *ignis fatuus* which has
deceived men. Rome, the anti-Christ—the accursed, Bible-
denounced, fire-doomed, citadel of the potentate "who sitteth
in the place of God, sheweth himself that he is God."

Were we to anticipate our subject and ask, And when shall
this system of error be destroyed? the reply is, *We cannot tell!*
Were it not for the unmistakable language of inspiration—
which points definitely to the period in which Rome must
inevitably perish—we should not have any basis on which to
establish the argument, that the system of the Roman hierarchy must perish. It has survived many a shock—it has
floated over many a tempestuous sea—it has navigated
through the convulsions of the mediæval ages—it has gone
triumphantly through the storm of the French revolution—
and, when every throne in Europe rocked—when every kingdom was shaken—she, recoiling like a wounded adder from
Napoleon's blow, reared herself again, and again hissed forth
her desolating poison, worse a thousand times than the deadly
shade of the Upas tree, by poets immortalized—again deluding
the masses who had for centuries groaned under her serpent-
like cunning, or dragon-like wrath. She was great when
Charlemagne bathed his sword in the blood of Italy—she
was great when Cœur de Lion led his mailed squadrons to the
walls of Damascus—she was great when Leo X. and Louis
XIV. ruled Europe—and even now, when universal science
and the light of the everlasting Gospel shine from every hill
and valley, is she less great than then—we answer, No!
Throned on the sea city of Venice, powerful in Italy, ruling
the court of Napoleon, governing Mexico, permeating the
masses of Europe, placing her crucifix in front of nearly every
American city: we have no proof drawn from her past history
or her present position that Rome will ever fall. Well might

he historian write *Immortal* on her front. Well might we imagine Rome impersonified, and giving the haughty answer to the question, " When, O, mother of harlots, wilt thou fall?" With one foot on the Vatican, with one in the palace of Napoleon, her left hand on Canada, her right embracing Mexico—her unblushing brow uplifted to those heavens which utterly repudiate her boasted pretentions; we can hear her scornfully replying to such a demand :—

" I *was* when your London was *not*,—I saw its rise—I will see its overthrow. I was old when the first Norman conqueror crossed the deep, and planted his standard on the cliffs of England; and I heard the song of Rollo, that pealed over the blood-red field of Hastings : I was old when the boasted Anglo-Saxon race was young: I saw its rise—I will see its fall. When Wesley and Whitefield ran their victorious career, I could point to my Chrysostoms and Cyprians a thousand years their elders : when the eagle of the American revolution " waved by the white sea foam, " and brooded over the political chaos of the New World, I had numbered twelve centuries; and could retrace my way through revolutions far mightier than these, the very recollections of which have been obliterated by the advancing waves of Time. I saw the first mariner who crossed the Atlantic : my arm launched his bark and trimmed his sail, when he crossed the then untraversed deep of the Atlantic. You ask *me when I shall fall?* I have outlived every other institution, religious and political : I have survived the storms of empires : I have stood undestroyed amid the overthrow of the dynasties of the past—and you ask me when shall I fall? When the world fails! Not *till* then—and not then.

" When stands the Coliseum Rome shall stand,
    When falls the Coliseum Rome shall fall;
    And when Rome falls, the world——

and even then Rome's religion shall not fall. By what right do you question my right to the name given to that city which is eternal? By what right do you assign to me a place mid scenes which are merely mortal? By what right do you point to a period in the future in which it shall be said, 'Rome was and Rome is not'—it can never arrive. By God established —by Christ defended—by a policy which is not human perpetuated, that period shall never arrive when the historian, standing on her ruined temples, shall say, 'Rome has fallen.'

'A world is at our feet, as fragile as our clay.'"

With deep, stern feeling—with intense expectation, the believer in revelation turns to the pages of inspiration; and says, I believe it, because it is written, "Babylon is fallen." With these words on his lips, he cares nothing for the boast, "I have lived a thousand years; I shall live a thousand years more." He points with unerring precision to the day when up to heaven shall ascend the victorious cry, "*Babylon—Babylon is fallen!*"

It is a painful task to contemplate human frailty—to contemplate fallen grandeur—a melancholy feeling is that experienced in looking over ruined Carthage and fallen Herculaneum, or to gaze on Thebes with her hundred prostrate gates, to blush over scenes of human desolation where once the tide of busy nations ran "in mingled pity or loud raised applause," but infinitely more distressing to the sentimentalist to gaze over fallen Rome, and the wrecked hierarchy. What a scene! The coliseum in ruins—the "owls long cry in the Cæsars' palace"—in the Vatican's halls! Where is the hierarchy? Dashed to atoms. "Verily! verily! of that edifice there shall not be left one stone upon another which shall not be thrown down." Babylon the great will fall.

As before observed, our present task will be to delineate this mystery of iniquity, viz: "THE SACRIFICE OF THE MASS."

To that one feature attention is demanded while we engage in its review.

I. We will show the meaning of a true sacrifice. II. We will give an outline of the Doctrine of the Mass. III. We shall show the Scriptural and logical objections making against the Doctrine of the Sacrifice of the Mass.

I. It is unnecessary here to enter into anything like an examination of the great logical theme—worship by sacrifice. We shall not even make a passing allusion to the Unitarian objection so frequently urged against the reasonableness of the glorious doctrine of the Atonement—the foundation stone of Christianity. We shall assume that all present believe in the doctrine of the sacrifice of Christ as being true. And that the sacrifices which characterized the early ages of our world's history are equally worthy of our belief, and typical of the coming of a Saviour. Let this be assumed, and we shall proceed to enter into the examination of the doctrine and nature of sacrifices and sacrificial worship.

No one acquainted with the history of our race will venture to deny that the first sacrifices were those offered by our first parents, immediately after the fall, and upon their expulsion from Paradise. If they were eucharistic, then the sacrifice of Christ was *not* by them prefigured—for *his* was propitiatory : if they were propitiatory, they doubtless referred to one great offering which Christ should make for sin in the fullness of time ; but as the christian doth, Romanist and Protestant are prepared to admit the *last* and deny the *first*—we assume at once that the sacrifice of Christ is propitiatory and atoning ; the great question follows, can there be more than *one* such sacrifice ? The Protestant answers, many, prior to Christ's one offering but none subsequently. Romanists answer—many *before*, and many *since*. Admitting fully—as we must do— that many sacrifices *preceded* the offering of the Redeemer, can it be shown that one ever *followed* him ? Since then the soul looks to his finished, offering as perfecting them forever who believe, with the termination of Patriarchal ages, came the introduction of the Jewish or Levitical system. Its character remained the same : typical of a coming Christ, who should be an offering for sin—altars were erected—fire was kindled—blood flowed—victims were slain—priests were established—and these prefigurative of the introduction of a system which should have fo¬ *its* central point " the Lamb slain from the foundation of the world."

We shall not dwell upon the objections which are marshalled by the shallow defenders of *natural* religion against the divine institution of sacrificial worship. Suffice for our present argument that the word usually translated " *sin*" in Gen. iv, 7, " if thou doest not well, *sin* lieth at the door" should be read " a *sin* offering coucheth before thy door"— (a lamb) which alters the meaning of the passage altogether. Every Hebrew scholar will admit that such is the correct rendering of the term ————— which means, according to the construction of the Hebrew, a " *sin offering.*" Thus then we have an express command from God himself to Cain, directing him for sin to make a sin offering. This sufficiently proves the divine origin of sacrifices as propitiatory, and as typical of the sacrifice of Christ. We will not here consider any of the objections. The death of the Holy one to whom spake God the Father in vision, was designed to be a sin offering even from everlasting. The effect produced by the *first* sacrifice must have been impressive and inspiring. They who had never seen, but had often heard of *Death* as the penalty for man's *sin*, see for the first time the flowing blood of the Slain Lamb offered in sacrifices—and hear the words " *This* is to die—this is DEATH."

We see, almost as soon as the waves recede from the slime of the post-diluvian world, the blood of sacrifices flowing—

and flowing by Divine *command*. Then we find sacrifices forming an important part of the religion of Judah. Altars were erected—priests were named—victims bled—men worshipped, believed, and were pardoned—and with these facts before us, we dare not deny the Divine origin of religious sacrifices. In the fulness of time, Christ the great sin-offering came—his propitiatory character was fully argued by the prophets, and endorsed by the apostles. To Christ as High Priest gave all the prophets testimony, " He was bruised for our transgressions—bruisedfor our iniquities : " again, " thou shalt make his soul a sin offering ".—" if," to use the words of Dr. J. P. Smith " the Scriptures are of any use to mankind," —if they convey any definite sentiments—if we can at all rely upon the meaning of the words—we must believe that the Messiah must devote himself as a voluntary sin offering, as a sacrifice for the sins of men. Of Christ's sacrificial character there can be no doubt." To go further—Daniel explicitly declares, that he was cut off for the sins of the people—in reference to this splendid prediction of the Messiah, it is admtted on all hands, that the express mention of the Messiah the Prince, excludes all doubt; nd its fulfilment in Jesus of Nazareth not *less* plainly established. By the agreement of the general description of the 70 weeks with his character, when dated from the 7th year of Artaxerxes Longimanus, terminating in the year of his crucifixion, the death of the Messiah is obviously meant by his being cut off—a phraseology which implies " a painful death at the hands of others," *Symington*. The design of the atonement manifestly is then to expiate before God for human sin—that being accomplished it becomes us to inquire—is there a necessity for the repetition of this great sacrifice there spoken of as by Messiah the Prince—or shall we regard *one* sacrifice as perfecting them forever who believe? To this *Protestants* answer, His *one* sacrifice requires no repetition. The Papacy answers, we must repeat it daily by the sacrifice of the Mass. It becomes our task, with whatever power we may possess, to show in the second place, that the views held by the Papacy on this sub- ject are incorrect. We shall now dwell upon the history of the doctrine of the Mass.

II. The Doctrine of the Mass. Many of our hearers have read the, descriptions of the ghosts in *Macbeth*,—you call after them, but there is no reply. So with the creations of Papal Rome,—you call after them, but there is no reply. A phantom is made to pass over the stage. We ask, whence dost thou come? Before a reply can be given, it passes away —and like the baseless fabric of a vision, leaves no wreck be- hind. From whence do we derive the dogma of the Mass? Let me draw attention to the doctrine, as laid down in the Romish Catechism :—

Q. Is the Eucharist a sacrament only?

A. No—it is also a sacrifice.

Q. What is a sacrifice?

A. It is a Supreme act of religion due to Almighty God.

Q. How is this performed?

A. By offerings made to Him, in token that he is the Sovereign Lord of all things.

Q. In what did the sacrifice of the old law consist?

A. Chiefly in bloody sacrifices of beasts, which the priests offered in the temple, as figures of Christ's sacrifice on the cross.

Q. In what consists the sacrifice of the new law?

A. In the voluntary oblation which Christ made to his Eternal Father, by dying on the cross for our redemption.

Q. How have we now any sacrifices of the new law?

A. By the standing memorial of it in the blessed Eucharist.

Q. Why do you say that the Eucharist is a standing memo- rial of Christ's death?

A. Because Christ, at his last Supper, commanded that it should be offered as a remembrance of his passion, to the end of the world; and this is what is performed in the sacrifice of the Mass.

Q. Why is it a continuation of Christ's sacrifice?

A. Because Jesus Christ, who is a Priest forever after the Order of Melchizedec, having offered himself once in a bloody manner on the cross, continues to offer himself daily thro' his priests in an unbloody manner, in the form of bread and wine. *Hence the sacrifice on the cross, and the sacrifice of the Mass are the same.*

Q. Who said the first Mass? A. Jesus Christ.

Q. When did he say it? A. At the last Supper, when he instituted the Holy Eucharist.

Q. To whom is the sacrifice of the Mass offered? A. To God only.

Q. What benefit do we receive from the Mass?

A. It is a daily application of the merits of Christ, and a daily laying before the Father the merits of his Son's bitter passion.

Q. What are the benefits the living receive by it?

A. They are many. It applies the merit of the Saviour's passion for the remission of sin.

Q. Does it help the dead? A. St. Augustine says, they receive thereby more mercy than their sins deserve.

In the Catechism legalized by the Emperor Napoleon, in 1806, the question "Does the mass avail for the souls of the dead?" The reply is—"yes—very much."

In the Catechism of the Council of Trent, we read :—"We confess that the sacrifice of the Mass is one and the same sacrifice with that upon the cross. The victim is one and the same—Jesus Christ. The bloody and the unbloody victim is still one and the same, and the oblation of the cross is daily renewed in the Eucharistic sacrifice, in obedience to the command of the Lord—'Do this in remembrance of me.'"

Hence, the Mass is termed by the fathers, an *incruental* or unbloody sacrifice. It is also called *latreutical*. It is also an *eucharistical* sacrifice of praise and thanksgiving. It is an *impetratory* sacrifice, by which we obtain whatever we ask. It is also propitiatory.

Throughout the Latin Church unleavened bread is used at Mass. There is certainly no scriptural warrant for this. There is no evidence to induce us to believe that in the Lord's Supper, during the Apostolic ages, the bread used was without leaven. The wafer is made thin and circular, and bears upon it either the figure of Christ, or the initials I. H. S. This is the real Christ of the Church of Rome, their God and Saviour, and object of worship.

Let me here narrate a story. It is related by the Rev. Edward Nangle, in one of his letters addressed to the notorious John McHale, Archbishop of Tuam. He says : " I am personally acquainted with a poor woman in this county who was delivered from Popery in the following manner. A friar one day came into her cabin, and, after the usual salutation had passed between them, he called for a sauce-pan. Placing the vessel on the fire with a little water in it, he took out of his pocket a vessel containing some flour, which he poured into the sauce-pan, stirring it, as though he were making stir-about. When the paste was thickened to the consistency of wax, he ordered his host to provide him with two smoothing irons ; and having pressed the paste between these instruments, to the thinness of a wafer, he cut it into round pieces with a pair of scissors, and then holding up one of the pieces, he said,— " When I have consecrated it, whosoever does not believe it to be the very soul and body, blood and divinity of the Lord Jesus, let him be accursed forever." It has been observed, that there is but a step from the sublime to the ridiculous. That step was taken. He broke the spell.

" The thought was so dreadful," said the woman, " that the flour he carried in his pocket, which I saw him boil in a sauce-pan, press out between two irons, and cut with a scissors, was God, that I resolved never to enter the Chapel again."

The poor woman adhered to her resolution. Romanists would be wise to follow her example. For however Dr. McHale, and his more talented Brethren in the ministry, may exhibit superior tact in the management of the wafer-idol, and cast a cloud of mystery round the wheaten deity, yet *their* God is no whit *better* than the friar's. " The workmen made it—therefore it is no God," Hosea viii. 6.

The robes used by the priests during the Mass, are of five different colors. The diversity dazzles. We love to look at the rainbow—

> " That airy child of vapor and the sun,
>   Conceived in crimson, cradled in vermillion,
>   Baptised in molten gold, and swathed in dun."

On the same principle, the eye loves the butterfly trappings of the priests, during the Mass. But then, in the one case we do look on the paintings of God himself : in the other, only on the tawdry trappings of human hands. *White* is used on all feasts of our blessed Lord, the Virgin—*Red*, on the Pentecost—*Green*, on all Sundays from Trinity to Advent—*Purple*, on all Sundays in Advent—*Black*, on Good Friday, and on all days when Mass is said for the souls of the dead. Popish authorities state that the linen veil, which the priest puts on, represents the veil put on Christ's face in the house of Caiaphas when they smote him. The *girdle* represents the cord with which the Saviour was bound, when seized upon by the Jews. The priest, before putting on the *maniple*, kisses the cross in the centre. And the *chasuble*, which is the last vestment which the priest uses, represents the seamless coat of our Saviour, and the purple robe in which he was betrayed.

Picture to yourselves, if you can, the mockery of this acting. A priest parading at the head of a congregation of worshippers who superstitiously believe, that by his puppet acting he is representing the crucifixtion of our blessed Redeemer. Common sense is outraged : and heathen rites are no whit more offensive to the reason and piety of mankind.

" There are always lighted candles on the altar during the Mass." But why ? Mass must be said in the fore-noon— w'.en the people do not want light ; and as the wafer-god has no eyes, he cannot require it. Why is the Mass celebrated in Latin ? The only reply to such a question, is that given by an Irishman,—" Sure the Devil does not understand Latin." It is a fanciful and irrational ceremony. I, does not honour God, or afford just views of Him : it does not humble man, and show him his sin—it does not exhibit the atonement and sacrifice of Jesus ; and amounts to nothing but a mass of self-contradictions, and self-evident absurdities. If I am asked, wherein is there a contradiction, I reply, that it consists in this—that while it is an axiom in Christianity that *there can be no remission without the shedding of blood,* (Heb. ix. 24,) the Roman Catholic maintains that in the *unbloody* sacrifice of the Mass, Christ is daily offered. There cannot be an unbloody sacrifice ! There never was since the creation : there cannot be, unless a new revelation proclaimed that God *could* receive such a sacrifice. In the sufferings of Jesus, God's justice was satisfied. He was crushed beneath a load of insupportable sorrows, under which he bowed his head and died. Now, in the Mass, will it be pretended that the sufferings of the Redeemer are to be repeated, and that the events of Calvary are to be re-enacted. He is ever and ever, when the Mass is performed, to descend from the midst of his glory and suffer again ? Where is the cross ? Where is the true body ? Where is the blood, and sighs, and tears ? Without suffering there is no sacrifice, and hence the Mass is a horrid blasphemy.

And let us here enquire, when did the sacrifice of the Mass begin? I shall not, in this paper, enter upon a minute enquiry as to the origin of this great error. It will be sufficient, if I demonstrate from their own writings that the sacrifice of the Mass did *not* begin with Christ and his Apostles. This is sufficiently evident. A great Cardinal, (Bellarmine,) and one whose authority no Roman Catholic would feel disposed to question, asserts, " the oblation which follows consecration, belongs to the integrity of the sacrifice, but not to its essence. This is proved from the fact that our Lord and his Apostles made no oblation at the beginning,"—that is, they offered a sacrifice without offering anything. But as the idea of a sacrifice is always connected with an offering of some kind, it is a palpable absurdity to argue that there can be a sacrifice without an offering. Such a doctrine bears its own refutation. Again, observe that Cardinal Baronius acknowledges that the Eucharistical sacrifice is an unwritten tradition, of which, consequently, there is no mention made in the Gospel. And he condemns the Council of Trent, for its assumed infallibility, by such an admission. Those references are of themselves sufficient to satisfy this and every enlightened audience, that at whatever time the sacrifice of the Mass began, it certainly did not begin with the Apostolic ages—but was the production of later times.

We shall now proceed to ask, what can invalidate or render the sacrifice of the Mass nugatory?

There may be defects in the bread. If it be not wheat, or if it be in the least degree tainted, it doth not make a sacrifice. If it be made of rose-water it doth not make a sacrifice. If it begin to corrupt, it may make a sacrifice, but the priest sins grievously.

There may be defects in the wine. If the wine be sour, then the sacrifice is not lawful.

There may be defects in the minister. If his intention be to consecrate but part of the wafers, the others are not consecrated.

There may be defects in the celebration. If, after the consecration, a gnat, or a spider, or any such thing fall into the chalice, he will either draw it out and burn it, or swallow it with the blood. If in winter the blood be frozen in the cup, let warm water be put round the cup till it be thawed.

Thus, then, we have briefly glanced at the two first heads of the subject, viz : I. the nature of sacrifice ; and II. the doctrine of the mass, as held by the Church of Rome. We have seen the first to be a Divine institution, rendered needful by man's sin. The second we have perceived to be a system of vast importance to the human family. One which, if true, we are bound to believe, as our salvation depends thereon ; but which, if not true, is the foulest piece of invention ever fabled since the fable of Saturn, who fed on the flesh of his children—a circumstance not more revolting than that men should literally *eat the flesh of their God.*

III. It now becomes us, if you will give me your attention for a little longer time, to dwell upon the refutation with which the doctrine of the sacrifice of the Mass may be met. I purpose first, then, to draw attention to the objections which are to be found in the Scriptures : secondly, to those objections which reason itself affords against a doctrine so monstrous and unmeaning.

The first objection then, which the Scriptures present to the doctrine of the Mass, is contained in the explicit declaration : " Christ by one sacrifice made perfect all things."— Heb. vii. I know not by what line of argument a defender of the Papacy can possibly elude the face of that passage.

There is no escape; and no shift nor subterfuge can avail. " By *one* sacrifice Christ perfects them forever who believe." That statement should be considered forever sufficient. The sinner is informed, by the Protestant Preacher, " By one offering Christ has atoned for the sins of men." The Priest of Rome tells him, " many offerings are required." If he appeals to the Scriptures, the question is settled. I defy any Roman Catholic to show from these writings, that the doctrine of a *repeated* sacrifice is mentioned, or in any degree, by the sacred writers, encouraged.

Another argument drawn from Scripture, against the absurd doctrine of a bloodless sacrifice, may be found in the consideration of the fact, that whoever sacrifices are mentioned, they at once involve the idea of the shedding of blood. Nothing can be plainer. The Apostle Paul's words are unmistakeable—" without the shedding of blood there is no remission." But the ministers of the Papal church maintain, that the mass is an *unbloody* sacrifice, in opposition to the *bloody* sacrifice of the cross. They would compel us to believe that a sacrifice without *blood* is the same as one wherein blood is shed; and that the vital fluid flowing from the Saviour's side, is the same as the purple tide flowing through uninjured veins—and that the torn body of Jesus on the cross is the same as the wafer lying on the table! For this Queen Mary lit the fires of Smithfield! For this we Protestants are given up by ex-communication to the bitter pains of everlasting damnation !!

By these two plain Scriptures, then, the doctrine of the Mass is overthrown. 1st—By the words " without the shedding of blood there is no remission ;" and 2nd—Christ " by *one* offering hath perfected them forever that believe." And if it can be shown that there is no blood shed in the many offerings of the Mass, we have argued to a demonstration that the doctrine of the Mass is unscriptural.

And now we ask, what do Romanists bring forward to support their doctrine? The fact that Melchizedec brought forth bread and wine to Abraham, has been adduced as evidence for the Mass oblation. They say he was a Priest—that he offered bread and wine;—consequently every true priest must do likewise. But to this it is objected, that there is no proof that Melchizedec's offering was sacrificial—it may have been an act of pure hospitality. And even admitting that Melchizedec did, in this bread and wine, offer sacrifice, it does not follow that the christian ministry succeeded that of Melchizedec. And admitting for the argument's sake that christian ministers are successors of Melchizedec, then does it follow that because *he* offered up bread and wine, that therefore they are to profess to offer up the body and blood, the soul and divinity of our Lord Jesus Christ? Certainly not: consequently the Romish Mass has no foundation in Scripture—but is violently antagonistic to the statements of the Divine Writings. They say, " lo! Christ is here!" And we are taught by Christ himself " to believe them not."

With this part of our subject the doctrine of transubstantiation is connected. But that doctrine would of itself form the substance of another lecture—and one which if the *present* should find favor with my auditory, and no better writer take it up—I shall freely give. I say that a few words on transubstantiation would be here very appropriate. I may be permitted to quote from the Catechism of the Church of Rome :—

Q. What is the Holy Eucharist?

A. It is a sacrament which contains the body, and blood, and soul, and divinity, of our Lord Jesus Christ, under the appearance of bread and wine.

Q. What happens by the words of consecration?

A. The bread is changed into the body of Jesus Christ—and the wine into his blood! And we find the following canon passed at the thirteeth session of the Council of Trent:

" Whosoever shall deny that in the most Holy Sacrament of the Eucharist, there are truly, really and substantially contained the body and the blood of our Lord Jesus Christ, together with his soul and divinity—and consequently Christ entire, let him be accursed."

We may add a word in relation to this dogma. It follows that by the virtue of five words—*hoc est autem corpus meum*, the bread and wine cease to be bread and wine, and become flesh and blood, and soul and divinity. And I am held accursed forever by the Church of Rome, if I will not believe a statement so monstrous! Well! I have no wish to deny to Christ's church the power to excommunicate under proper circumstances; but under these circumstances it amounts to this, that Rome has consigned the bodies of men to the fire, and their souls to hopeless perdition, for refusing to believe that which bears the self-evident marks of falsehood and contradiction.

Time does not permit us to enter fully upon the argument against the doctrine of transubstantiation. But if it did, we should perceive it to consist in a statement such as this: " To the law and to the testimony, which is your own Protestant rule. Christ hath said of the bread, *this is my body*, and *therefore*, such it certainly is, whatever our *senses* or *reason* may say to the contrary." I know not if there be a Roman Catholic Priest within these walls. There may be. If so, he will admit that I am putting the question fairly—and he will also corroborate my assertion, than the argument before us they have nothing higher.

But the facts are against them. For be it so, that the bread was substantiated into flesh, that was not Christ's own flesh which was eaten, but newly created flesh. But that which Christ took he broke—that which he broke he blessed —that which he blessed he distributed, and what he distributed, was eaten. But *bread* was broken by Christ—consequently it was bread and not flesh which was eaten.

The Priest in giving the wafer says " Behold the Lamb of God who taketh away the sins of men." The communicant says, " Lord, I am not worthy that thou should come under my roof." He then shuts his eyes, and receives the wafer on his tongue, saying, " Amen! I believe it to be the body of Christ—and I pray that it preserve my soul unto eternal life."

And is it possible that there are men in our midst who would introduce again such absurdities into our country! And these men, some of them, once Protestant! I respect the honest man who changes for conscience sake—but who can have sympathy with a Judas! a Julian! or a Maturin!

It was said by David—" Thou wilt not leave my soul in hell—neither wilt thou suffer thy Holy one to see corruption." But if the doctrine of transubstantiation be true, His body perpetually undergoes corruption.

Again—Christ says, " the poor you have always with you, but me you have not always." If the soul, and body, and divinity of Christ be in the wafer, then it is not true that He is not always present. He is certainly always present.

IV. Lastly, we will turn to some of the logical absurdities which flow from the doctrine. Then let me enquire, from what other infallible source can we derive knowledge than the evidence of our senses? But our senses testify, that after the words have been employed which transubstantiate the bread and wine into flesh and blood, that they still remain bread and wine. The *sight*, the *smell*, the *sense*, the *touch*, all concur in their testimony as to the fact that no change has taken place in the elements, but that they still remain simple bread and wine.

Another absurdity would flow from the admission of this doctrine. Far be it from me to make difficulties where none exist. But here the absurdity is obvious. The humanity of Christ could not be proved, if the doctrine of transubstantiation be true. The Marcionites thought Christ's body to be only a phantom, consequently they denied the incarnation. How easily might those say to the Church of Rome, if you believe that the bread is only bread in appearance, but in reality, flesh : we, on the same reason, state that the body which hung upon the cross was only a body in appearance, and was no reality.

Another absurdity flowing from this admission of the doctrine of the Mass would be found in the conclusion, that upon every celebration of the Mass the Son of God must descend from the throne of his glory, and again be offered as a victim ! Can any reasonable mind admit so monstrous a doctrine ? Would Cardinal Wiseman himself defend it ? What ? that although it has been sung in heaven, when Jesus ascended on high, leading captivity captive—

> " Unfold your bars of living light,
> And let the King of Glory in ;
> He claims those realms as his right :
> The victor over death and sin,"—

that he must descend again ? Again engage in the travail, and anguish, and sweat, of the tree of the cross, and be pierced afresh, so often as a Priest offers up the wafer-god as a sacrifice, to appease or turn away the wrath of an offended God ? There cannot be conceived a greater absurdity. Reason grows weary in the attempt to reconcile so monstrous a paradox as the real presence at the sacrament.

Did time justify the attempt, I would proceed to show that the Fathers, so called, are universally against the doctrine of the real presence at the sacrament. Ignatius, Ireneus, Justin Martyr, Origen, Clements, Cyprian, and Eusebius, unite in their testimony against the real bodily presence of Christ at the sacrament, and from the doctrine of his real bodily presence. These venerable men all unite to contradict the present monstrous doctrines of the Church of Rome, as regards the real presence of the Redeemer in the sacrament of the Mass.

With what face dare a Roman priest assert that the testimony of the Fathers is in favor of the sacrifice of the Mass? With the universal testimony of primeval ages against him, in vain—in vain can they claim the support of antiquity.

We are on the eve of a period in which the great drama of Rome must be wound up. Events are hastening to their consummation. The last act of the drama is about to take place—and very soon of Rome and her religion will it be said —she is among the things which have passed away. Long has she occupied the principal place of the earth. No poet will embalm her in verse, as Byron baptized pagan Rome, when exclaiming—

" The Niobe of Nations," &c.

The men are living to-day who will see the overthrow of the Papacy. And when she is gone, the nations will be again permitted to breathe with freedom. No one who has given any degree of attention to the study of Fleming, or Dr. Clarke, can doubt but that the destiny of Rome is near. " When the fig tree putteth forth its leaves, then know ye that summer is nigh—even at the door." So with the fall of Babylon—she is near her end : she totters to her fall. And even now the cry is heard, " Come out of her my people, that ye be not partaker of her plagues."

I am not eloquent—but what though I am not? The light of the sun, mellowed in glory and loveliness, may diffuse its richness over the dim blue mountains, and summer fields, and sparkling streams, when he himself is not visible. His light is refracted from the opaque moon. So with the light of the long ages which are gone, it may come reflected through as dark a medium as the soul which is now flashing over yours some of the best thoughts of the Ref—mation. It matters not what be the medium, so long as t! . . at be shed abroad which shall inspire men to higher and holier purpose, and nobler performances.

The farmer sows wheat; it grows, it ripens, it is reaped, and is prepared for the mill, where it is ground, and sifted with a sieve; with part thereof the fowls are fed—with a part man is fed—but that is not God. A part is brought forward and laid upon the altar—but yet it is not God: the priest handles and crosses it, and yet it is no God: he pronounces a few words over it, and immediately it becomes the Supreme Jehovah. He falls down and prays to it, saying, "Thou art my God:" he lifts it up before the people, and cries—"*Ecce agnus dei qui tollit mundi peccati*"—"Behold the Lamb of God who taketh away the sins of the world:" the whole congregation fall down and worship it, crying, "*Mea culpa, mea maxima culpa*"—"My fault, my great fault."

By what right dare he assert this to be God, which yesterday was bread? By what right dare he excommunicate my soul from the joys of heaven, because I believe not a doctrine so monstrous. By what right dare he demand that a Protestant should bow in the dust till the elevated host pass by? God has not given that right. Man repudiates it! and devils mock at it—whilst angels weep over such moral obliquity—and were it not that he has forgotten to blush, the Priest himself would be ashamed of a pretension so utterly baseless!

Yet, though mingling in the dense purple clouds of her superstition, the twilight of the Church of Rome has pierced through the hazy ages which have passed away. To her are we indebted for the preservation of the inspired writings. But for her we had not received the experience which comes from other times. But her sun is veiled—and its beams, if they do not pierce to our common humanity, are the scorching lightnings of a wrong zeal—not the warmth-giving glow of a heavenly religion. If she shines, it is with the light of a meteor—not that of the sun. She strikes—but she crushes the friends of Jesus, and the enemies but too frequently escape. She smiles, but her smile as often falls upon vice as upon virtue. She has beauty and power—but it is the beauty of Lucifer, the fallen son of the morn—of whom Byron cries—

> " Save he who made him,
> Who ever was like Lucifer!"—

Her power—it is the power of Apollo Belvidere—if we could imagine Apollo Belvidere, in all his unearthly loveliness and power, sightless and erring. Every element of beauty and power is embodied in that glorious form—but look we more nearly and the eyes are wanting—the strong and beautiful one is blind. And Rome is beautiful and strong—but Rome, too, is blind. She has eyes, which are sightless.

And now, for the evening, my task is done. I have endeavored to redeem my promise of showing the nature of a sacrifice, the doctrine of the Mass, and the objections which may be urged against that doctrine. I am conscious that I have very imperfectly discharged my work: but " he does well who does his best." I have endeavored to do the best I could. I may have offended some whose apprehensions are keen of expecating Rome. But to them I would just say— our quarrel with the Papacy is irreconcilable: it is a war of utter death to one religion or the other. Between God and Satan, Christ and anti-Christ, can be no harmony—there can never be but war until one or the other be destroyed.

And, in closing, allow me to say that I rejoice at the formation of the Protestant Alliance. Accused as that institution has been of political motives, it is nevertheless the offspring of Protestantism and religion. I trust that the institution will still continue. It is linked with all that is grand and glorious in history. We boast our connection with Huss, with Jerome, with Luther, with Melancthon, with Cranmer, with Knox, with Latimer, with McBride, with Chalmers, with

Cumming; and although the destruction of the Alliance has been threatened, yet we say :

> "———— Sail on !
> 'Tis but the flapping of the sail,
> And not the rent made by the gale.
> Despite of false lights on the shore,
> The breakers dash, the tempests roar;
> Despite the rocks beneath our lea,
> Our faith triumphant, all our fears,
> Our hopes, our expectations, tears,
> Are all with Thee ! are all with Thee ! !"

I shall close by quoting from Pollock's inimitable and immortal " Course of Time," the apostrophe to Rome :—

> " *As yet had sung the scarlet-colored whore,*
> Who on the heart of civil power reposed
> Her *harlot* head—the Church a harlot then,
> When first she wedded civil power,
> And drank the blood of martyred saints ;
>   Whose priests were lords,
> Whose coffers held the gold of every land,
> Who held the cups of all pollutions full,
> Who with a double horn the people pushed,
> And raised her forehead full of blasphemy
> Above the Holy God, usurping oft
> Jehovah's incommunicable names :
> The nations had been dark, the Jews had pined,
> Scattered without a name beneath the curse ;
> War had abounded : Satan reigned unchained
> And earth had still been black with moral gloom.
> And now the cry of men went up
> Before the Lord, and to remembrance came
> The tears of all His saints—their tears and groans.
> Wise men had read the number of the name ;
> The prophet years had rolled—the time, and times,
> And half a time, were now complete.
> The seven fierce vials of the wrath of God,
> Poured by seven angels strong, were shed abroad
> Upon the earth, and emptied to the dregs.
> And lo ! another angel stood in heaven,
> And cried aloud with mighty voice—'Fallen, fallen,
> Fallen is Babylon the great, to rise no more ;
> Rejoice, ye prophets, over her rejoice ;
> Apostles, holy men, all saints rejoice,
> And glory give to God and to the Lamb.' '
> And all the earth and heaven said, Amen !"

Mr. Chairman, my task is done. May the God of the Reformation be our God forever.